Tales from Celtic Lands

To Robin Isaac Berk and to all the Children of Memory — C. M.
To Johnnie and Rita with love — O. W.

Barefoot Books
2067 Massachusetts Avenue
Cambridge, MA02140

First published in the United States of America in 2003 by Barefoot Books, Inc.
This hardback edition first published in 2008

This book was typeset in Stempel Schneidler (13pt on 22pt leading) and Celtic Hand
The illustrations were prepared in watercolour and ink on 140lb watercolour paper
Graphic design by Judy Linard, London
Colour separation Grafiscan, Verona
Printed and bound in China by Printplus Ltd.

This book has been printed on 100% acid-free paper

ISBN 978-1-84686-213-7

The Library of Congress catalogued the hardcover edition as follows:
Matthews, Caitlín, 1952 –
Celtic Memories / told by Caitlín Matthews ; illustrated by Olwyn Whelan.
—1st ed.
p. : cm.
Summary: An illustrated collection of traditional Celtic stories, blessings and rhymes,
accompanied by notes on each story and a guide to pronounce the Celtic words used.
ISBN 1-84148-097-5
1. Celtic literature – Adaptations – Juvenile literature. 2. Celts – Juvenile literature.
(Celtic literature – Adaptations. 2. Celts) I. Whelan, Olwyn. II. Title.
823/.914 21 [F] 21 PR6063.A8625C45 2003

135798642

Tales from Celtic Lands

Retold by Caitlín Matthews

Illustrated by Olwyn Whelan

Barefoot Books
Celebrating Art and Story

CONTENTS

THE MAGIC OF MEMORY

These stories were first told a long time ago when people didn't, or couldn't, write their tales down: they told them aloud, and passed them on to their descendants, who learned them by heart and told them to the next generation. Nowadays, we are so used to writing everything down that we find this idea strange, but when we have to depend on memory, our brains work in a different and more efficient way. Indeed, when we are young and don't have so many facts stored away in our memories, our brains are often a lot livelier than when we are older.

The stories that we hear when we are young stay in our memories far longer than the stories that we read to ourselves, so ask your parents or teachers to read these aloud to you. (If they have problems saying the names, a guide on how to pronounce the Celtic words is given in the notes about the stories at the end of the book.) When you listen, close your eyes. You will be experiencing exactly what your ancestors did: pictures, images and scenes will spring up in your imagination, which some people call "the mind's eye." When you want to think about that story again, the things that you will remember first will be the pictures that came to life when you first heard it; it is these images that help you bring the story back. This is a trick that all actors, singers and performers quickly learn, because it is the easiest way to remember long scenes, songs or stories.

Some of the descendants of the Celtic tribes still live today in Wales, Scotland, Ireland, the Isle of Man, and Brittany in France. In the olden days, the bards, who were poets and musicians, were responsible for telling stories to the Celtic people. They recited aloud the tales that people needed to remember. Starting when they were children, the bards learned hundreds of stories, songs and poems. When they were grown-up, they had the equivalent of a small library in their memories. People valued their storytellers back then. In the long dark winter nights, when people couldn't go outside, but had to do all their indoor winter tasks – like mending buckets, plaiting ropes, carving spoons – they listened to stories and sang songs together. They also shared riddles, tongue-twisters, sayings and puzzles.

When Celtic people had problems, they would say prayers or blessings, and recite charms asking for help from the spirits of the natural world, from their ancestors, or from God, depending on what they believed. They felt that people who had died weren't lost forever, but could still hear and help them. The fairies who lived in the woods, valleys and secret places, weren't imaginary, but real neighbors who could help them – as long as they treated them with respect and didn't ignore them or make them angry. They believed that the spirits of the mountains, streams, seas and trees were alive, and they had their own stories and songs. As people's beliefs changed, our ancestors still remembered these unseen neighbors in their stories, songs and prayers. The stories in this collection are like that – people's ordinary lives are interwoven with magical encounters with fairies, spells, enchantments and help from miraculous sources. This is the magic of stories – not the magic of magicians, but everyday magic, which is part of everyday life and doesn't only exist in a separate world.

Some people say that nowadays magic has disappeared, or else they say that magic is bad, but I think that they are wrong. Modern stories ought to have enchantment in them to remind us to look for the magic in our own lives. It seems strange, in a time when there are so many new stories written and when nearly every home has a television, that there is so little magic in books and television programs. If people tell you that magic is for children, what they are really saying is, "I remember the magic from when I was young, but if you want to be grown-up, then you had better forget all that and live in the real world." It's really very sad, because the truth is that everyone needs some magic in their lives, however old they are.

The best defenses against becoming a dull grown-up are a good memory, a quick wit and a loving heart. These will keep you interesting all your life, whatever you look like and wherever you live. And if that's not true, may my fingers grow into twigs for the birds to nest in and my tongue become a razor-strop for the wit of the fairy rhymer!

Caitlín Matthews
Oxford, January 2003

THE LADY
FROM THE LAKE

WELSH

O nce upon a time, near Llanddeusant in South Wales, there lived a poor
widow with her only son, Rhys. The only thing they owned was a small
herd of cows. Each spring, when the new grass waved green, Rhys would drive
the cattle up into the Black Mountains so that they could graze and make sweet
milk. His mother would turn it into butter and cheese.

The cows' favorite pasture was right next to Llyn y Fan Fach or the Lake of
the Small Peak. Early one morning, Rhys saw a beautiful woman sitting on the
surface of the water, combing her long, golden hair and looking down into the
lake, using the water as a mirror. It was clear that she was not like the girls of
the valleys with their work-reddened hands, for this lady's fingers were fine
and white, and her face was full of ancient wisdom, though she seemed young
and lovely. Since Rhys had been about to have his breakfast, he held out the
barley bread and cheese toward the lady.

She put her head to one side and came toward him over the water, looking
at the bread as if she had never seen any before. Rhys saw that the bread had

been badly burned down one side, but he could not withdraw his offer now. The lady said, in a clear bell-like voice,

Your bread is well baked indeed!
But it's not so easy to catch me.

And with that she dived under the water. Rhys was heart-stricken, for he had fallen deeply in love with the lady at first sight. He thought to himself that he must have offended her by offering her burnt bread. The next morning he tore off a piece of half-risen bread-dough as it sat rising by the warm fire, and before milking his cows, went off to the lake.

Again, the lady appeared, and Rhys offered her the moist piece of half-risen dough. The lady came nearer and looked at it, saying,

Under-baked is the bread you hold!
I cannot take you, my good soul.

Rhys was deeply saddened, for he longed for the lady with all his heart. The next day, with high hopes, he took a loaf of bread that was completely cooked but not overdone and burnt. This time, when the lady appeared, Rhys stepped into the waters of the lake and offered her the bread. She looked at it and then at him, saying with a merry smile,

Good is the bread you give to me!
But will loving promises last always?

Rhys blushed and stammered out his love to her, asking her to be his wife.

The lady said to him,

Bride I will be, by your side I will stay,
But strike me three blows and I'll quickly away.

"I will never, ever strike you," Rhys promised. But much to Rhys's disappointment, she dived back under the waters. He was about to turn home, thinking that his wooing had all been for nothing, when he saw three people emerge from the lake. There was an elderly man of noble appearance and two ladies, both looking exactly the same. The old man greeted Rhys politely. "Which of my two daughters is the one you love? If you can choose the right one, then I will gladly consent to your wedding this very day."

Rhys looked and looked, but not a hair of difference could he tell between them. He was about to give up and guess when he noticed that the one on the right had moved her foot forward very slightly. And it was then that he noticed that the two daughters had fastened their sandals very differently. He gestured to the lady on the right and said, "This is the one for me."

The old man of the lake nodded his head, "You are right indeed. Now, you must be a kind and faithful husband to her, and I will give my daughter a

dowry of as many animals as she can count without drawing breath."

The old man called out, "Sheep!" and out of the lake onto the shore there came a line of sheep. The lady started to count, "One, two, three, four, five. One, two, three, four, five. One, two, three, four, five," over and over, until her breath ran out.

Rhys thought to himself, "They cannot have to count very much in the land beneath the lake if they can never count beyond five," but he kept his thoughts to himself in case he would appear rude.

Then the old man called out goats, horses and cattle while his daughter counted. When she had finished, the mountain pass was full of beasts which she and her new husband drove down to the valley.

Having so many animals made Rhys very prosperous. He was able to move to a new farm near the village of Myddfai, where he and his wife lived happily for many years with their three sons. Rhys's mother lived long enough to see and

play with her grandchildren before she died, happy to see the family's fortunes restored and to see the great love that was between Rhys and the strange woman he had brought down from the mountain to be his bride. The lady from the lake might say little, but she was a good mother to her children.

Now, one day there was to be a christening party some distance away to which they were invited. The lady was reluctant to go because it was too far to walk.

"Then you must take a horse from the field and save your legs," said Rhys.

"I'll do that," said his wife, "but you must fetch my riding gloves from the house," for she still needed to keep her fingers fine and white.

Rhys fetched them and came out again to find his wife still standing there. "Must I do everything?" he muttered to himself, but to the lady he said, "I've brought your gloves. Go on, go on, fetch the horse then!" and playfully struck her with the gloves. The lady drew herself up and looked upon him sadly, saying,

> *New life's beginning, the start of all care;*
> *Forgetful of blessings, a long road to fare.*
> *Bride I have been, by your side I will stay,*
> *But strike two more blows and I'll quickly away.*

And Rhys remembered his promise, though he had not meant to break it by striking her with the gloves. He promised to be more careful in the future.

A few years passed and they were invited to a wedding party. Everyone was singing, dancing and making merry when the lady burst into tears right in the middle of the room, to Rhys's great astonishment. She was crying so hard that she was upsetting the good cheer of the party, and Rhys clasped her shoulder very firmly and shook her to stop, asking what was the trouble. She said, weeping,

Sorrow is guest at this wedding feast,
Troubles begin, soon dancing will cease.
Bride I have been, by your side I will stay,
But strike one more blow and I'll quickly away.

And Rhys remembered his promise again, for he had struck his wife for a second time, without meaning any harm to her. He apologized to his hosts for the upset and took his wife home, resolving to be more careful in the future.

The years passed and their sons grew up. Rhys was careful not to offend his wife in any way and to think of her needs before his own. They loved each other so very much that it would be a terrible thing to strike her, even by mistake, for then she would go away forever.

Now, one day they were invited to a funeral party. It was a very sad occasion, with everyone sitting woefully around, weeping and speaking respectfully about the old farmer who had died. Suddenly, in the middle of the sad quietness, the lady burst into merry laughter and could not be made to stop until Rhys reached out and clutched her wrist quite roughly, "Wife, wife! Be still!" But the lady continued laughing, saying,

Troubles cease when we're freed from life,
The coming of death is the end of strife.
Bride I have been but can no longer stay;
By three blows your promise has withered away.

And, at that moment, Rhys knew that he had broken his promise for the last time and that there would be no more chances.

Without another word, the lady rose up and went home where she started to call together the animals that were the descendants of the sheep, cows, goats and horses which had come out of the lake with her.

> *Come brindled, white speckled,*
> *Come spotted and freckled,*
> *From four fields white-sided,*
> *By the old white-face guided,*
> *And the gray milk-taker,*
> *With her white bull maker*
> *From the court of the king,*
> *And the black calf roast*
> *That spits and toasts:*
> *Come hither, come homeward!*

And all the cows immediately came to her, even the black calf that had just been

slaughtered and put to roast over the fire. They all got up and followed her. As she strode up the mountain, she called to the four oxen ploughing in the high field,

And the four oxen gray,
From fields come away,
Come hither, come homeward!

And the yoke and harness pulling the plough fell from their backs and they trotted after her, along with the cows, goats, sheep and horses who followed her, one by one, back into the lake.

Rhys stumbled home, unable to speak, and sat by the fireside, a broken man. His three sons traveled all over the Black Mountains, searching for their mother, but they could not find her. The family by the village of Myddfai now fell on hard times. They could no longer boast of their rich farm, when they had no beasts upon it.

The eldest son, Rhiwallon, missed his mother as much as he feared for his father's sanity. Almost a year from the day she had disappeared, she appeared to him while he was walking upon the mountains. Rhiwallon was overjoyed to meet her again. He tried to persuade her to return to them, but she refused, saying,

From the lake I bring healing to mortal men,
That life's good gladness they might know again!
This wisdom of healing I give to my line,
By word, herb and blessing as health's own sign.

She gave to him a bag of herbs and remedies, and instructed him on how they were to be used. Rhiwallon thanked her and went down to the valley where his father was, meaning to tell him everything that had happened. But when he saw how sad his father looked, he remembered one of the remedies that his mother had given him for those whose minds have been unsettled. He made a porridge out of linseed, putting betony, aloe-wood, fennel and anise seeds into it, and fed it to his father. After a few days of deep sleep in a darkened room, Rhys recovered his mind and was much calmer about his wife's leaving.

Rhys lived for a few more years and, when he died, his soul rejoined the lady from the lake who had been his wife. As for Rhiwallon, he became a famous physician and healer, passing on his skills to his three sons Cadwgan, Gruffudd and Einion. People called this family "the Physicians of Myddfai," for they each did their best to heal the people of Wales. After many hundreds of years, the remedies of the lady from the lake were written down in a book, so that they might be shared with other people – but no healers were as good as the Physicians of Myddfai. Members of that family are still living in South Wales, proud to know that they are descended from the lady from the lake.

A Blessing For When You Get Up

May I arise today under the strength of heaven,
under the light of sun,
under the radiance of moon.

May I arise with splendor of fire,
with the speed of lightning,
with the swiftness of wind.

May I arise supported by the depth of sea,
by the stability of earth,
by the firmness of rock.

May the nine fold powers
surround and encircle me
above, below and about.

Traditional Irish Blessing.

THE BLACK BULL
OF NORROWAY

SCOTTISH

Long, long ago in the land of Norroway, there lived a woman who had three daughters. As they grew older, they longed for households of their own. One day, the eldest daughter said to her mother, "Bake me a bannock and roast me some meat, Mother. I am off to seek my fortune." And the eldest daughter went to the old wise woman who could tell the future. The wrinkled old wise woman looked into the girl's hand and into her face and told her to look out of the back door and tell her what she could see. The girl looked three times, and on the third time a covered coach drawn by six white horses jingled down the road. She ran in and told the wise woman, who said, "That's the one for you!"

And the eldest daughter was taken into the coach and away she went.

Now, the middle daughter, too, grew weary of her solitary life, and she sighed and said, "Bake me a bannock and roast me some meat, Mother. I am off to seek my fortune." And away she ran to the wise woman, who looked into her hand and into her face and told her to look out of the back door. She looked three times and there she saw a farmer's wagon drawn by four brown horses.

"That's the one for you," said the wise woman, and the middle daughter got up onto the wagon and away she went.

Now, it was dull at home for the youngest daughter, who said to her mother one weary day, "Bake me a bannock and roast me some meat, Mother. I am off to seek my fortune." The old wise woman looked carefully into her hand and searchingly into her face and told her to look out of the back door and tell her what she could see.

She looked once, twice and thrice, and what should she see roaring along the road but a great black bull. She ran and told the wise woman who said, "That's the one for you," and, to the girl's great terror, lifted her onto the bull's broad back and away they went.

Long they traveled and on they traveled and no harm had come to the girl, but she grew very hungry, and couldn't repress a groan. The bull heard her and said, "Eat what you find in my right ear and drink what you find in my left ear." Trembling, she reached into his great right ear, where she found a loaf of good bread. From his left ear, she drew out a flagon of ale. Putting aside her fears, she ate and drank and felt very much better.

Long they traveled and on they traveled until night drew its cloak about them and they could go no farther. At the side of the road was a castle where they stopped. The bull said, "We will stay here for the night, for this is the place of my brother and we will be welcome."

Servants ran out and pulled the girl off the bull's back, for she had ridden so long that her legs would no longer work. They put her in a fine room, and in the morning the bull's brother came to her. He was in the shape of a mortal man. He spoke to her kindly and gave her an apple, saying, "Good lass, take this apple and keep it safe by you. I urge you not to open it until you are in the worst trouble that a mortal can suffer, and it will help you."

And the lass was lifted onto the great bull's back and away they went again. As they rode, she began to wonder about the bull and why he didn't look like his brother.

Long they traveled and on they traveled until the sun dropped out of the sky like a stone and they could go no farther in the darkness. At the side of the road was a castle where they stopped. The bull said, "We will stay here for the night, for this is the place of my second brother and we are expected."

Servants ran out and helped the lass off the bull's back, and drew her to the fire. They put her in a fine room and in the morning the bull's second brother came to her. He, too, was in the shape of a mortal man. He spoke to her kindly and gave her a pear, saying, "Take this pear and keep it safe by you. Take care not to open it until you are in the worst trouble that a mortal can suffer, and it will help you."

Once more she was lifted onto the great bull's back and away they went. As they rode, she wondered about the gifts she'd been given, and what help they could give.

Long they traveled and on they traveled until the wind blew snow against them and they could go no farther in the growing cold. At the side of the road was a castle where they stopped. The bull said, "We will stay here for the night, for this is the place of my third brother and here we can rest."

23

Servants ran out and helped the girl down from the bull's back, brushing the snow off her. They put her in a fine room and in the morning the bull's third brother came to her. He was also in the shape of a mortal man. He spoke to her kindly and gave her a plum, saying, "Take this plum and keep it safe by you. Make sure not to open it until you are in the worst trouble that a mortal can suffer, and it will help you." And they lifted her onto the black bull's back and away they went.

Long they rode and hard they rode until they came to a dark and menacing glen, where the bull stopped next to a large stone so that the lass could step off his back.

The bull looked earnestly into her face, saying, "Stay here while I go and fight with my enemy. Sit on this stone and move neither hand nor foot till I return, or you'll never see me again. If everything turns blue about you, then I will have been victorious. But if everything turns red, then he will have vanquished me, and you will have to make your way homeward alone."

The girl stroked his head and wished him luck, and then sat and trembled quietly inside herself, trying not to move as the bull disappeared into the dark

glen. There came terrible sounds of fighting, groaning and striking, but she could see nothing. After a while the air around her turned blue. She was overcome by joyful relief that the bull had won and she clapped her hands together.

In that instant, everything slowed. The air shimmered, the waters stopped flowing in the mountain burn, the birds no longer flapped their wings, the grasses no longer waved in the wind. She blinked and blinked, and when she opened her eyes, she was still sitting on the stone, but she and the stone were somewhere completely different. She began to cry, because she realized that the bull wouldn't be able to find her now. She would have to find him instead!

She slipped her hand into her pocket and felt the three fruits that had been given to her. Perhaps she should break one open, for surely this was a terrible thing to happen to anyone? But then she thought more carefully; she was unharmed and still able to look after herself. Perhaps this was not the time to call for help?

She looked about her and saw a smooth hill made of glass, which seemed to be the way that she should go. She walked right around it, seeking for a pathway up, but wherever she tried to climb, she slid straight down again.

She came at last to a smithy where the blacksmith was hammering out iron.

"Blacksmith, can you make me a pair of iron shoes with spikes on the soles so that I can climb the glassy hill?"

"I can indeed," said the blacksmith. "What payment will you give me?"

The girl had nothing but the three fruits in her pocket and she considered giving him one of these, but something made her stop. She was sure that the fruits had been given to her for a much worse situation than this. "I have nothing," she said, sadly.

"Iron shoes with spikes are difficult and expensive to make," said the blacksmith. "If you serve me for seven years in the forge, then I will call that a proper payment."

And so for seven years she worked in the forge, learning all that the blacksmith could teach her, and at the end of the time she was given the iron shoes. She fastened them on and ran straight up the hill without stopping.

At the top there was a single cottage belonging to a washerwoman who lived there with her daughter. "Seldom do we see travelers in this land," said the washerwoman. "But two in one week is most strange! Just last Thursday there came a gallant young warrior with his shirt all covered with blood,

needing my help. He had come from the wars and was sorely wounded." What the washerwoman didn't tell her was that the warrior had said that the woman who washed his shirt clean would be his bride. But though the washerwoman and her mean-spirited daughter had washed until their fingers were sore, they couldn't shift the bloodstains.

The girl's heart turned over when she heard about the wounded man.

"Where is the warrior now?" she asked. "He is resting in the back room, and needs much tending. I am so behind with my washing, perhaps you could help me?" said the wily washerwoman, who gave the girl a basket of washing, including the bloody shirt.

The lass took the basket down to the bubbling waters of the burn, where she soaped and scrubbed and wrung until the washing was all clean, including the warrior's shirt. The washerwoman was delighted when she saw the clean shirt and took it to the warrior and told him that her own daughter had washed it.

That evening at supper the washerwoman announced that, as soon as the warrior was entirely recovered, he and her daughter would be wed. The food stuck in the girl's mouth when she heard this news, and her heart grew heavy. She had never felt such sorrow before. She reached into her apron for a hand-kerchief and her hand touched the apple. Now was the time to use it, she was sure! She went to her room and broke it open upon the floor. Inside it was full of gold and diamonds.

She went to the washerwoman's mean-spirited daughter and offered her the gold and jewels, saying, "If you will let me sit with the warrior this night, I will give these to you."

The washerwoman's daughter greedily snatched up the treasure but she told

her mother what she had agreed. Her mother made up a sleeping potion to give to the warrior. Just before the brave lass went to sit with him, the warrior drank up the potion and fell deeply asleep. The lass tiptoed into the room and looked upon his face for the first time. On the bed lay a young, black-haired man with lines of suffering etched upon his face, but she knew from the lurch of her heart that this was her beloved black bull restored to his own shape. All night she sat by him, holding his hand and singing,

> *Seven long years I served for you,*
> *The glassy hill I climbed for you,*
> *The bloody shirt I washed for you,*
> *Will you not answer and turn to me?*

But he never stirred all night.

The next day she was in despair, so she broke open the pear, which was filled with silver and pearls. She went again to the washerwoman's greedy daughter and offered her the silver and jewels in return for a night tending the wounded warrior. But again, the washerwoman gave him a sleeping potion and he slept through the whole night. The brave lass was desperate, for her weeping and singing did nothing to rouse him. Over and over she sighed,

> *Seven long years I served for you,*
> *The glassy hill I climbed for you,*
> *The bloody shirt I washed for you,*
> *Will you not answer and turn to me?*

The next day the warrior was feeling much better after his long, deep sleep and he called for a man to shave him ready for his wedding on the following day. One of the men who cut wood for the washerwoman, and who lived in the room below the warrior's, came and shaved him. He asked him, "Did you not hear the strange song on the wind last night? I could swear it was coming from your room!"

The warrior resolved to stay awake the next night and see what it might be.

Now the brave lass drew out her last hope, the plum, and dashed it onto the floor. From its heart spilled out precious rubies and emeralds. She ran with them to the washerwoman's surly daughter and begged to be allowed to tend the warrior on the night before his wedding. And again the washerwoman brought a sleeping potion to the warrior just before bedtime. This time, he pretended to sip it but said it was too bitter. While the washerwoman went for a pot of honey to sweeten it, he poured out the potion upon the floor and, turning over and pulling the bedclothes up, he pretended he had drunken it anyway.

The brave lass went into the chamber and sat with him once again, singing her song,

> *Seven long years I served for you,*
> *The glassy hill I climbed for you,*
> *The bloody shirt I washed for you,*
> *Will you not answer and turn to me?*

The warrior turned toward her and said, "I hear and answer you, my brave soul! Love of my heart, will you be my wife? For it was you who washed my shirt clean and lifted the enchantment that was upon me by your patient courage."

Then he took her into his arms and kissed her.

They made their way down the glassy hill, away from the old witch of a washerwoman and her mean-sprited daughter, past the blacksmith's smithy and back into their own country where they lived happily forever and ever.

Summer Welcoming Song

Golden summer of the white daisies,
Here we come bringing summer in.
From village to village and home again after,
Here we come bringing summer in.

May-time dolls and summer maidens,
Up to the hill and down to the glen,
Girls in their dresses, white shining, adorning,
Here we come bringing summer in.

Larks lift their song, on blue skies go threading,
Blossoming trees are laden with bees,
Cuckoos are calling, the birds joyful singing,
Here we come bringing summer in.

At the cliff's edge, the hare it is resting,
Herons nest high in the sway of the branch,
Doves they are cooing, the honey is streaming,
Here we come bringing summer in.

Shine of the sea lights the long-covering darkness,
Silver the shore reflects glittering sea,
Dogs they are barking and cows they are lowing,
Here we come bringing summer in.

*Traditional Beltane song from Northern Ireland, translated by Caitlín Matthews.
In Ireland, children carry around a Beltane doll dressed in ribbons to welcome
in the summer. Beltane is another word for May Day.*

THE BOY WHO DIDN'T KNOW

BRETON

Once a very long time ago in Brittany there lived a noble lord. Riding along one day, he found a small boy asleep by the roadside and he asked him, "What are you doing there?"

"I don't know," said the boy.

"Well, who are your father and mother?"

"I don't know."

"What are you called and where are you from?"

"I don't know," the boy answered to every question.

The lord decided to raise the boy himself and called him N'oun Doaré, which is Breton for "I don't know." He gave N'oun Doaré a good education and, when the boy was nearly twenty, the lord took him to the big fair in Morlaix.

"Whatever work you choose," said the lord, "I will buy the tools that will help you to be successful in life."

N'oun Doaré wandered through the fair, looking at this and that. He didn't know what kind of work he would most like to do, but he had the idea of

becoming a knight. He kept returning to a scrap-metal stall, where there was a rusty old sword. "Buy me this, please," he said.

The lord was disgusted. "It's red with rust and of no use whatsoever." But, true to his word, he bought the sword.

N'oun Doaré polished it up and discovered an inscription. "I am invincible" it read under the rust. The boy smiled and tied the sword to his waist.

"I need a horse," he then said to his protector. They searched the market, looking at all the livestock. The fair was closing up when N'oun Doaré spotted the one he wanted. It was a thin, starveling mare that looked near to death.

"That's the one for me," he said, and begged the lord to buy it. While his protector was counting out the money for the mare, the old Cornishman who was selling it whispered to N'oun Doaré, "See these knots upon the mare's halter? When you untie one of these, the mare will take you many hundreds of miles distant to where you want to be."

N'oun Doaré thanked his master and mounted the mare. When they were out of sight, he undid one of the knots and, without any notion of where they

might go, he and the horse arrived in Paris. This was obviously the place where he would make his fortune, and so he went to the king's palace and was given work in the stables. Whenever N'oun Doaré had a day off, he would untie one of the knots and see where the mare took him, and many adventures they had together. On one of these, when he was riding home, he passed through a village he had never seen before. There, shining at the crossroads, was a golden crown, glittering with diamonds.

"What a beautiful thing," breathed the boy.

"Beautiful but dangerous," said the mare. "Leave it alone."

N'oun Doaré couldn't quite believe that the mare had spoken, so he slipped the crown under his coat and rode homeward, where he used it to light up the stables at night; it was forbidden to take any flame into the horses' stables lest they catch fire.

All went well until a jealous groom ran with tales to the king.

"My groom has a better crown than myself," said the king, much put out by the whole matter. And he demanded that the crown be brought to him. The king asked, "Where does it come from?"' but N'oun Doaré couldn't tell him.

All the wise men of the kingdom examined the crown and admitted it was the finest they had ever seen, but they couldn't explain its origins. Then  the thin, starveling mare, who was behind them, whispered, "This is the crown of the Princess of the Golden Ram."

No one knew who had spoken, but the king sighed with love as her name was mentioned, and he peered at the diamond-studded crown with great longing. "I must marry that lady! You! N'oun Doaré! This is all your fault. I command you to find the princess and bring her here to me, or I will kill you."

N'oun Doaré wept into the mare's mane with fear and anxiety.

"Did I not tell you to leave the crown alone?" said the mare. "Well, now that the trouble is here, we had better do something quickly. Ask the king for a sack of oats and some money, and we will find the princess for him."

"You really do talk!" cried the boy, glad that his instinct to buy the mare was proving right.

The king gave him oats and money, and away they rode until they came to the seashore. There they found a fish stranded by the tide, and close to death.

"Quickly, put the fish back into the water!" whinnied the mare, and N'oun Doaré did so.

"Thank you, N'oun Doaré," bubbled the fish. "I am the King of the Fish. If ever you need my help, come to the edge of water and call me and I'll come."

Farther along the road they came to a clearing where a bird had been caught in a snare.

"Quickly, release the bird!" whinnied the mare, and N'oun Doaré obeyed her.

"Thank you, N'oun Doaré," sang the bird. "I am the King of the Birds. If ever

you need my help, call me on the winds of the air and I'll come."

They rode over mountains and rivers, through forests and valleys, until they came to the golden walls of a mighty castle where they heard a tremendous bellowing. As they approached, they saw that there was a man chained to a tree. Upon his body were as many horns as there are days in the year.

"Unchain the man quickly," whinnied the mare, but N'oun Doaré hesitated. "I daren't go near him for he is quite ferocious."

"He will not harm you, trust me!" said the mare, and so the boy unchained the horned man who said, "Thank you, N'oun Doaré. I am the King of the Horns. If ever you need my help, call from any part of the land and I'll come."

The mare told N'oun Doaré to go into the castle and ask for the princess, and then invite her back into the woods to see his dancing mare. So while the mare grazed, in went N'oun Doaré. "I want to speak to the Princess of the Golden Ram," he said.

The princess was welcoming and showed him her castle of wonders. N'oun Doaré looked around politely, and then said, "I have a wondrous mare, who knows all the dances of Brittany. Would you like to see her?"

The princess ran out to the woods, clapping her hands with excitement. N'oun Doaré said, "She will be glad to show you her dances if you get upon her back, sweet princess."

And he helped her mount and climbed up behind the princess and undid a knot of the halter. Away they flew, back to Paris.

"You've tricked me!" cried the princess, beating her hands together with anger. "I shall make you suffer before I'll be wed to the King of France!"

N'oun Doaré brought the princess to the king, who exclaimed over her perfection, and begged her to marry him.

"I cannot marry you unless I have the ring that lies in my bedchamber. I made a solemn promise to my dead mother that I should wear her ring on my wedding day," said the princess stubbornly. "But the ring is locked in the little chest and the key has been lost."

The king commanded N'oun Doaré to fetch the ring or else be put to death. N'oun Doaré ran to the stables to ask the mare to fly over the miles so they could fetch it, but there were no more knots left upon her halter. N'oun Doaré had made too many adventurous rides. Now he wept.

"Remember the King of the Birds!" whickered the mare in his ear.

And N'oun Doaré called into the winds of the air, asking the King of the Birds to help him.

"Please can you fetch the ring in the castle of the Princess of the Golden Ram?"

And the King of the Birds called all the birds together and asked the smallest one to undertake this quest. Only the tiny wren was small enough to fly into the keyhole and bring the ring back in his beak, though he lost a few feathers doing so.

N'oun Doaré brought the ring to the princess, who stamped her foot and said to the king, "I still cannot marry you, unless I have my own castle brought here and set down facing your own, for I am a powerful princess in my own right, and I cannot live in the palace of my husband."

The king commanded N'oun Doaré to fetch the castle or else be put to death.

"However can we do that?" he cried to the mare, who tugged at his tunic, saying, "Remember the King of the Horns?"

So N'oun Doaré stamped upon the earth and summoned the King of the Horns to help him fetch the princess's castle. And the King of the Horns called together all the horned beasts of the earth and bade them assist him in drawing the castle back to Paris where, the very next morning, that castle stood, facing the palace of the King of France.

When the sun rose and struck the golden walls of the castle, the people leapt out of bed shouting, "Fire! Fire!," they were so bright and glowing.

"Now we can be married," said the king.

"Oh, no!" said the princess. "I don't have the key to my castle and I can't let you in without it. The key is a magical key which no earthly locksmith can make again, for the old one dropped to the bottom of the ocean."

The king commanded N'oun Doaré to fetch the key or else be put to death. He leant against the thin, starveling mare and cried with fear, for he couldn't swim.

"Remember the King of the Fish," whickered the mare into his ear.

So N'oun Doaré went to the water's edge and yelled down into the waters for the King of the Fish, who called together his fish and made them search for the lost key. Finally, a salmon rose to the surface with the diamond key in its mouth, and N'oun Doaré took it to the princess.

She could no longer pretend that there were any reasons to delay, and she and the king went to church to be married. Amid the rejoicing and celebration in the square outside, N'oun Doaré stood with his mare. As the bells rang out to proclaim that the princess was now the king's wife, the skin fell off the thin, starveling mare to reveal a beautiful dark-haired woman.

N'oun Doaré's mouth fell open with surprise as the woman said, "I am the daughter of the King of Tartary, and I have been under a spell of enchantment. Of all the men in the world, I would choose you to be my husband, for you have helped release me from the spell. Will you come and be the king of my country?"

"'Very gladly," said N'oun Doaré, taking her hands.

And the king was so very happy with his wife that he knighted N'oun Doaré with the same old sword that came from the scrap-metal stall in Morlaix. But as he was about to pronounce the words, "Arise, Sir N'oun Doaré"' the rust fell from the blade, and the sword sang out, "Arise, Sir Invincible."

And somewhere in Tartary, they say, King Invincible still lives with his bride, and whenever he needs to know anything, it is his wife who always has the right answer!

A Blessing For Travelers

May the road rise to meet you.

May the wind be always at your back.

May the sun shine warm upon your face,

The rains fall soft upon your fields

And, until we meet again,

May you be held safe in the palm of God's hand.

Traditional Irish blessing.

THE CAILLEACH
OF THE SNOWS

SCOTTISH

Once upon a far time, when there was water where there is now land and
land where now there is water, there lived the Cailleach, old and ancient
beyond reckoning. She had seen more years than any other being upon earth.
For her, the winters were her nights and the summers were her days. It was
the Cailleach who had formed the mountains when she and her sisters first
came to the land of Scotland, long before people lived there. They flew over the
land, throwing stones from their aprons and where these stones fell to earth,
great mountain ranges sprang up.

Many centuries passed and the Cailleach and her sisters grew tired and
weary. A younger race of people came and lived on their land, and the Old
Ones withdrew to the high mountains where they could not be disturbed by
the doings of human beings. Now, the reason why the Cailleach and her sisters
had survived for so many years was the secret Well of Youth, high up in the
mountains. Whenever the pains of old age came upon them, they would bathe
in those clear, cold waters and emerge fresh and young again. But since the

coming of people, the waters of the Well of Youth would only rise at certain times. Soon it became clear that there would only be enough water for one of the sisters to bathe in.

The sisters said, "Let us draw lots between us and see which of us will bathe when the waters rise again." The lucky sister would go into the well and emerge youthful again, while the remaining sisters would grow ever older and more infirm. Gradually, the sisters grew older and older until they could no longer remain upon the earth. They did not die as humans die, but would sit still, looking out over the lochs and pastures of the lowlands until each one turned to stone. One by one, each of the sisters became a part of the mountain ranges that they had helped to form, returning to stone, until only the Cailleach was left.

The Cailleach mourned her sisters, crying, "Hoo-a hoo! Where are my sisters now?" Her tears became snow and her sighing became the winter gales, and the land fell under snow and ice.

After that sad time, the years hung heavy upon her. Hers was a lonely life.

While her sisters were alive, they would want for nothing, for each did her part. The sisters would hunt for and prepare food; they would do the washing, make clothes and sing strange and haunting songs together when darkness fell. Now there was no one to help her, and the Cailleach became as grim as an icy morning when the sun never rises out of the clouds.

She managed her life as best as she could. She clothed herself with the veils of the weather: cloaks of starry nights, cloaks of clear blue days, robes

44

of gray, knitted clouds. Her boots were of reindeer leather from the many herds of reindeer that covered the land of Scotland in those days. They drew her chariot and provided her with meat and milk. When she wanted to wash her clothes, she tossed them into the whirlpool of the Corryvrekin, and the swiftly spiraling waters threw them back to her when they were clean.

When her bones ached and her strength began to fail, she would bathe in the magical well, which renewed her, although no one would call her young. The waters did not have the power that they once had, and they rose too seldom to restore her to full youth and beauty. At the rare times of their rising, she would have to ensure that she was the first to reach the waters, before a bird drank there, or before a dog barked.

Her life became perpetual winter. As the years turned, she would shun the warmer months of summer and hide within the sunless valleys of the high mountains, between the secret and mysterious places of the high, jutting rocks. But when the winter returned, then she would stir and go about. With her stone hammer, she would strike the ground until it grew hard with frost. Not a blade of grass could grow once her hammer had fallen.

At the approach of spring, the Cailleach sat upon the mountain lamenting her lost youth, "Hoo-a hoo! Where now are the happy days with my sisters?" Every breath of her sighing became a mighty wind that gathered upon the air as a dark, frowning cloud. People would say to each other, "The Blue Hag is crying for her sisters," and the fishermen would fear going out to sea in case her sighing blew up storms when they were far from shore.

Age hung upon the Cailleach as snows cloak the heights of the mountaintops. Years passed like days, days like seconds. When she went to the Well of Youth, there was always less water in it than there had been before. When she bathed in the waters, she emerged less youthful, less agile. The tasks she had once performed easily now grew harder. She needed a servant to tend to her needs: a maiden to fish the lochs, to weave her clothes, to prepare her food and comb her hair. From all over Scotland, she stole young women to be her servants. She chose the nimblest, strongest and most beautiful maidens, snatching them from their homes and families to tend her. But the Cailleach lived so long that, one by one, the maidens she took to be her servants grew old and died.

People were fearful of letting their young women go out alone in case the Cailleach took them, for she grew cunning as the years passed. Winter had

become the time of her strength when she was able to go about in the form of different animals, as a monstrous sow, as a narrow gray wolf, as a slippery eel, or as a querulous crane.

Now, there was a girl by the name of Bride who lived in the house of a druid with her mother, who was the druid's servant. Bride would look after the sheep, following them over the hills. The druid gave her a bone whistle, saying, "When you are in the high passes, keep this whistle around your neck, for the Cailleach seeks a new servant and she can take many shapes. If you see a monstrous sow, or a narrow gray wolf, if you become aware of a slippery eel or a querulous crane, then blow this whistle and my protection will be yours."

One day Bride went up into the hills with the flock, and a thick, icy mist came down so that she lost her way. She called out to the old bellwether sheep that led the flock. Hearing the sound of hoofs upon the rocks, she stretched out her hand and touched – not the thick woolly coat of a sheep – but the greasy, leathery skin of a pig. She quickly put the whistle to her mouth, but before she could blow it, she was snatched up and carried off by the Cailleach, who had been laying in wait for her. The whistle fell invisibly into the icy mists.

The Cailleach bore Bride back to her drafty cave and set her to milking the herd of deer that were penned in the glen. Many hundreds and thousands of years had passed since reindeer roamed these glens, and now there were only the red deer of the mountains. Bride, who had been used to milking the sheep, now tended the deer and instead made cheese from their milk. And always she dreamed of home.

The seasons passed, and though Bride searched for the lost whistle, she never could find it. One day, the Cailleach took the form of a crane and took Bride down to the seashore to fish with a baited line. "Fill this creel with fish before nightfall," commanded the Cailleach. "I shall feed along the loch side and fetch you back before dark."

With shivering fingers, Bride baited the line with worms and wept, longing for her mother. As she cried upon the sea-shore, a black and white bird with a long red beak drew steadily nearer, calling, "Klee-ee, klee-ee!" It was the druid who came to her in the shape of an oystercatcher. "Keep fishing, Bride, and listen to me! I have been searching for you for the better part of a year. The time of the Cailleach is passing, and the time of Bride is coming. Do as I say and not only will you be free from the Cailleach's service but you will also inherit her wisdom and power. She cannot survive many more winters without renewal."

"What must I do?" whispered Bride, taking the fish off the line into the creel.

"Three things will bring you freedom. First of all, you must discover her secret name, then you must discover the Well of Youth; lastly you must overcome her iron grip upon winter so that the spring may speedily return. To find out her name, you  must ask her how long she has lived. Listen carefully to all that she tells you and report it to me, for I will come to you again."

Later that evening, Bride made up the fire and gave the Cailleach a beaker of deer's milk, saying shyly, "You must have lived a very long time, great Cailleach."

"Ah, child! I have lived from before the time when the seas were once land and the land was once water. Before the mountains raised their peaks, and the glens filled with lochs, the Daughter of the Bones was born," said the Cailleach sadly and would say no more.

The oystercatcher came to Bride once again and listened to what the Cailleach had said. "The Cailleach's secret name is 'Nic Neven,' the Daughter of the Bones," said the transformed druid. "Armed with this knowledge, you will be able to find the place of her secret renewal and ensure that she cannot use it. The time is near when she must renew herself or perish. Watch and follow her closely. But now you must gather rushes from the loch and weave them into this shape," and the bird drew in the earth with its beak, making a threefold starry wheel. "You will need this starry wheel to seal the well until the Cailleach goes to her long sleep," and the bird taught her what to do.

When the Cailleach dozed in her cave, Bride's busy fingers wove the starry wheel from the rushes she had hidden. The very next day, long before dawn, the Cailleach went in the shape of a narrow gray wolf to inspect the well, and Bride followed her at a distance. But the time for the waters to rise had not yet come and the Cailleach-wolf slunk away down the mountain. Bride went to the well and, just as the druid had taught her, she laid the starry wheel woven out of rushes upon the opening of the well and said,

In the name of the ancient one, Nic Neven,
I seal this well with the star of heaven.
By spark of sun and ray of fire,
May the waters of youth rise up no higher,
Until I call with voice of power;
Then waters rise and mountain flower!

Bride said to the oystercatcher, "I have done all that you told me, but how can her iron grip upon winter be loosened?"

The druid-bird said, "Cut a birch wand from the tree that grows at the head of the glen and teach the Cailleach the Dance of the Mill Dust. It is many hundreds of years since she danced and she will be delighted. You must show her all the steps and movements and, putting the birch wand in her hand, tell her that she must first practice upon you. Make sure that you fall down first

and let her strike your hands, feet and mouth with the wand. When she does that, then you will be dead for a short time. But never fear, for I will be nearby to whistle the music. Be firm and brave, for she will want to dance in turn, and she will breathe upon your hands, feet and mouth so that you become alive again. When it is her time to fall down, you must strike her with the wand upon her hands, feet and mouth, and then she will become like stone and all her power and wisdom will be yours. But you must be sure never to breathe upon her hands, feet and mouth for, if you do, she will awaken again."

Bride cut the birch wand and hid it under her cloak. Later that night, she went to the Cailleach, saying, "The nights are long without dancing and music. I wonder whether you would like to dance, great Cailleach?"

The Cailleach sighed, "Hoo-a hoo! It is long since I danced with my sisters upon the first grass of the glens. I am too old now and we have no music."

"I've thought of that. I've taught this bird the tune of a dance – it's the only one he can whistle."

The oystercatcher obediently whistled the Dance of the Mill Dust with its jaunty rhythm. The Cailleach's foot began to tap and soon she was begging to be taught the dance.

Bride brought out the wand from the woodpile and showed the Cailleach how the dance went. "First we come together, then we step away, then we weave and change places," she explained, banging the birch wand upon the ground to the rhythm of the steps. Soon the Cailleach was breathless. "It's a very vigorous dance!"

Bride smiled. "Yes, but we take turns having a rest – like this. First one of us taps the other on the head with the wand and the other falls down. Then the one who is still standing will touch the other on the hands, and they do a little dance of their own; then the feet and lastly the mouth. And then when the one on the floor is very still, the other one breathes onto their hands, feet and mouth and they stand up again and change places. Have you got your breath back now? Well, why don't you try holding the wand and I will lie down first while you're learning the dance. Then, you can take your turn lying down and rest as long as you like."

"Good!" said the Cailleach. And they began. First, she tapped Bride on the head and down she fell to the floor. With the wand, the Cailleach made Bride's hands and feet do a little dance of their own while she lay upon the ground, her heart pounding with fear. She trusted the druid, but she didn't know whether the Cailleach would remember to breathe upon her hands, feet and mouth again. For if she didn't, then Bride would be dead forever. Then the Cailleach tapped her on the mouth with the wand, and Bride felt the breath dry up within her. The oystercatcher whistled on, but Bride heard no more until the Cailleach began to breathe upon her mouth, and the life came back into her and she leaped up gladly.

"Now it's your turn to dance!" said the Cailleach, and they began again. This time, Bride struck the Cailleach with the wand and she fell to the ground so that the earth itself shuddered. The wand made the Cailleach's hands and feet do a little dance of their own, which made the needles on the pine trees tremble and the icicles hanging from the rocks begin to shiver. But these were the last movements that the Cailleach made, for when Bride touched her mouth with the birch wand, the Cailleach turned to cold, unmoving stone.

The oystercatcher bowed his head to Bride, saying, "The power of the Cailleach is now yours. Use the wand wisely, for, as the light lengthens, so the cold strengthens."

Bride felt that great power within herself and promised then and there to be the helper of all beings who were in trouble. She called out in a loud voice,

Nic Neven's power is overthrown!
Rise up, waters, from deep-down stone!
By ray of fire and spark of sun,
May winter's whiteness be undone!
Life be renewed by springtime's power;
Now black ice crack and mountain flower!

Bride raised the wand, and the starry wheel of rushes that covered the Well of Youth flew into the sky like a spinning sun. The waters of the well swept up onto the power of her song and fell as rain upon the land of Scotland, melting the ice and snow. Upon the mountainside, the first green shoots of snowdrops pierced the hard ground, and everywhere people gave thanks and welcomed Bride back among them.

Every year, we still remember the coming of spring by weaving Bride's cross out of rushes, to celebrate the turning wheel of the sun of the seasons, and to remind us to call upon Bride when we need help. And to this very day, the oystercatcher is known as Gille Brighid, or Bride's Servant.

The winters are not so hard as they once were, and the Cailleach rarely moves from her confinement of stone. But, if the snows sweep down from the high mountains and cloak the land with white, people still say the Cailleach of the Snows walks the land once more.

New Year Carol

Joy, health, love and peace
Be to you in this place.
By your leave we will sing
Concerning our king.

Our king is well dressed
In silks of the best.
With his ribbons so rare,
No king can compare.

In his coach he does ride
With a great deal of pride
And with four footmen
To wait upon him.

We have traveled many miles,
Over hedges and stiles,
To find you this king
Which we now to you bring.

Now Christmas is past,
Twelfth Day is the last;
The Old Year bids adieu,
Great joy to the New!

Welsh – Pembrokeshire Wren Song. At midwinter, in South Wales, where Pwyll and Rhiannon lived, (see "The Mysterious Claw"), a wren was chosen to be King of the Birds and carried around in a little cage by boys who would collect food or money and sing this song at each house to bless the coming year.

THE SLAVE WOMAN'S SON

IRISH

There was once a mighty king of Ireland called Eochaid, the Lord of Slaves. He was known as this because he captured so many slaves from the coast of Britain. One of these captives was the beautiful, black-haired Cairenn, who was the daughter of King Scal of the Saxons. Now Eochaid fell in love with her, but did not make her his wife, because his queen and chief wife, the lovely Queen Mongfind of the Fair Hair, would have screamed and shouted with jealousy. As it was, Mongfind set Cairenn to the cruelly hard work of carrying water. You may wonder why the king allowed such a thing to happen, but the truth is that Mongfind was a witch who kept Eochaid so much under her thumb that some people called him the "Slave King" behind his back.

A year later, Cairenn bore King Eochaid a son called Niall but, because Cairenn was a slave, her son was not treated like a king's son. Mongfind forced Cairenn to work hard from sunrise to sunset, drawing heavy buckets of water from the well, and she had to leave her baby alone, carefully wrapped up in a basket, while she worked.

One day, a poet called Torna was passing by and, hearing the baby crying, he took him into his arms and rocked him. Now, in those days, poets were also prophets who could foresee the future. The moment Torna touched the child, he knew Niall's destiny. Cairenn came hurrying from the well.

"Is the boy yours?" Torna asked.

"Yes, he is Niall, son of King Eochaid, Lord of Slaves," said Cairenn. "But his father will never acknowledge him because, although I am a king's daughter, I am only a slave in this land."

She said this so sadly that Torna's heart was touched. The poet put the baby into her arms, and asked, "Daughter of the Saxon King, will you entrust your child to me? As his foster father, I will raise him as the son of a king and a queen and educate him myself. For I tell you that this boy is destined for great things. He will rescue you from slavery."

Cairenn had lived long enough in Ireland to know that poets spoke the truth. Kissing Niall farewell, she gave him into Torna's keeping.

The years passed and Niall was brought up to learn all the skills expected of a prince. Torna took care to speak often of Cairenn, his mother, as well as to prepare Niall to meet his father. When that day came, Niall and Torna made their way to Tara, the palace of the kings of Ireland. Before they entered under the royal

ramparts, they passed the well where they met Cairenn carrying a yoke with two heavy buckets of water.

"Niall, that woman is your mother. Go and greet her!" whispered Torna.

Niall could not believe his eyes. He lifted the heavy yoke from her shoulders, throwing it to the ground in disgust. "Mother, I swear that you shall nevermore do the work of a slave!"

Cairenn was overjoyed to see how strong and tall her child had grown.

"But, son, I dare not stop because of the queen."

"You shall be a slave no more!" said Niall firmly, and he took his mother to his own house and wrapped a cloak of royal purple about her shoulders, so that everyone should know to treat her as a king's daughter.

When Mongfind heard that the beautiful British slave had stopped work at the command of a poet's foster son, she flew into a fury. She entered the hall just as Torna was presenting Niall to his father. Eochaid ignored his wife, looking tenderly upon Niall and loving him for having the courage to defy Mongfind.

"The way that you honored your mother was the true deed of a king's son," said King Eochaid, who had grown very tired of the four lazy sons whom Mongfind had given him. "In the presence of this court, I recognize Niall as my son. He shall be given honor equally with his half-brothers."

The queen could scarcely believe her ears. These alarming words threatened the future of her own sons. But she kept her counsel and said, craftily, "My husband, the years flow past us and we must make plans for when we are both gone. It is surely time for you to decide which of your sons should succeed you as king when that day comes."

Eochaid was delighted that Mongfind seemed to accept Niall so readily. The question of who should be king after him could easily be settled now that Niall had come to Tara, he thought, but the queen had other ideas.

She was determined that one of her own sons should be the next king, and as everyone knew, the queen always got her own way.

The king turned to the poets to settle the question. Torna said to the king, "Under our law only the very best candidate can be king. With boys who are not yet men, it is difficult to tell who will become wise, strong and just enough to be the ruler of Ireland. Why not send Niall and your four other sons to be tested by the smith, Sithchenn. He is known by all as a wise servant of truth. He will surely discover which of the lads is fit to be king."

And so the boys were sent to help Sithchenn in the forge. He was a huge, silent man who could hammer out molten metal with his bare hands.

All the boys were set to work, to fetch and carry and do the chores so that the smith was free to make the finest weapons in the land. Mongfind's lazy sons soon saw that they would not be able to shirk their duties, as Sithchenn noticed all that the boys did and the way that they worked, though he said nothing.

While the boys were all hard at work in the forge, Sithchenn silently took a flaming brand from the fire and thrust it unseen into the thatch overhead. As the black clouds poured down, filling the forge with choking smoke, the boys began to panic, but Sithchenn called out calmly, "Rescue what you can!"

One by one the boys looked around for something to carry out to safety. Tall Brian, the eldest, seized the hammers. Anxious Ailill brought out an armful of weapons. Fat Fiachra lifted out the pail of beer and some bellows. Feeble Fergus grabbed some firewood, but only Niall had the forethought to carry out the anvil. Smeared with smoke and panting, they looked up for the smith's approval of their quick actions, but Sithchenn only had eyes for Niall.

"This boy knows what is most important in times of danger. What is a forge without its anvil?" he said to the other boys. "The rest of you brought away things that can easily be replaced. Because of this, you will be replaced by this lad. If you are wise, you will befriend Niall, for he will be king, not you."

Mongfind refused to accept Sithchenn's decision. She demanded that a second test be made. King Eochaid said to the smith, "I do not doubt your word, but I ask you to set one final test so that everyone is sure."

Sithchenn looked levelly at the king, "I can do no more. Let the boys be tested by the land itself, for the land over which the king rules should choose a worthy ruler."

Before dawn of the next day, Sithchenn blindfolded the five boys and led them into the heart of the deep, ancient forest. Once they were completely lost, he told them, "This night you must fend for yourselves with no one to tell you what to do, and with no slaves to wait on you. I shall come and find you tomorrow."

The five boys watched fearfully as Sithchenn's massive form disappeared into the dense woodland. They had no supplies and no weapons, except a little knife at their waists.

"What shall we do now?" wailed Feeble Fergus, who had never had to do anything for himself before.

"I'm hungry!" Fat Fiachra complained, for none of them had had any breakfast.

Anxious Ailill peered into the forest darkness, "Are those the eyes of wild beasts?"

Tall Brian said bravely, "We must do the best that we can."

Niall focused upon their most immediate needs. "We must make spears to defend ourselves and hunt for food."

Mongfind's sons did not much like Niall, but this seemed a sensible suggestion, so they each sharpened the end of a piece of wood and began to organize a hunt. They had never been hunting before by themselves, so they missed spearing many animals because they chattered together or because they noisily snapped twigs when they walked.

It wasn't until they started to work together, when it was nearly dark, that they managed to run down an elderly deer and drag it back to their encampment.

Brian was able to get a fire going and his brothers skinned and jointed the deer for cooking. None of them had ever done this before, since it was usually the work of slaves. They were surprised at how messy and bloody they had become. "We need water," said Niall.

Feeble Fergus was sent to fetch water in the deer's skin, since he was useless at cutting up the meat. After much searching, he finally came to a clearing where he heard the sound of trickling water. There was a spring bubbling up but, seated beside it, sat a terrible creature – an ancient woman who guarded it. Her skin was black as coal, her hair like a horse's mane. Her teeth and nails were green as forest leaves. Her body was scrawny and spotted. Her eyes glittered like a snake's.

Fergus fell back in horror. Forgetting his manners, he said, "You are surely the ugliest woman in Ireland."

The old woman cackled, "I am indeed. But I am the guardian of this well."

Fergus remembered his manners and bowed. "Old woman, may I have some water?"

"You may, if you give me a kiss upon my cheek."

Fergus considered her hairy, scabby cheek, and said, honestly, "I would rather die of thirst than kiss you." And off he went back to the camp without bringing any water. His brothers were angry with him and Fiachra went to try. Again, he met the old woman, but was too squeamish to kiss her. He, too, came back without any water and it was Ailill's turn. He soon came running back, scared out of his wits. Then Brian went to the spring, but he thought himself too handsome to kiss an old hag.

Finally Niall went to the spring. His foster-father, Torna, had taught him always to be respectful to women, but even his heart shrank when he confronted the old guardian of the spring.

"Do you wish to have water, Niall?"

He was surprised that she knew his name. "I do."

"Then you must first kiss me on the cheek before you drink."

Niall drew nearer and, closing his eyes, pressed his lips to her warty cheek. But his lips touched smooth flesh and he opened his eyes to see a very different woman before him. Her skin was fair and young. Her hair was golden and shining. Her teeth were like pearls and her lips and nails were stained with red dye. Her body was straight and supple.

Her eyes considered Niall with warmth.

"You are the most beautiful woman in all Ireland," Niall exclaimed. "But who are you?"

"I am the Goddess of the Land, O' Niall who will be King of Tara," said the woman.

"Were you under enchantment that you looked so ugly before I kissed you?" he asked.

"No, Niall. I came here to test you and your half-brothers. Though many wish they could be kings, the duties of a king are hard and difficult. A new king takes on his kingdom as it is, however difficult its problems; if he does his very best for his land, then he will find that to be a king is glorious and rewarding. Take the water that you came for, but refuse to give any to your half-brothers until they accept you as the next king."

"I thank you, lady," said Niall, bowing to the ground before the radiant Goddess of the Land.

He washed the bloody deer-skin farther down the stream until the water ran first red and then clear. He dipped the skin into the spring as it flowed from the earth and drew up clean water. When he looked up, the Goddess was gone.

He carried the water back to the camp where the four sons of Mongfind waited miserably. There was a light and determination about Niall that made them draw back.

"You may drink from this skin only if you accept me as the next king of Tara."

Bloodstained, muddy and thirsty, his half-brothers laid their makeshift weapons at his feet and Brian spoke for them all. "You won the test at the forge, Niall, and you have shown yourself superior today. We will be your loyal followers when you become king."

Sithchenn led them back the next day and the whole story was told to the king. Mongfind demanded to know why none of her sons had accepted the test of the Goddess of the Land, but they merely shook their heads, ashamed to remember how badly they had behaved.

Sithchenn answered her, "The Goddess of the Land knew that only the rightful heir would recognize his future wife, for he who is king must love his land as if it were his wife. None of your sons were worthy to wed such a wife and so they have forfeited their rights to be king."

King Eochaid embraced Niall. "As Niall will be my heir, it is only right that his mother should live with us here." And he ordered that Cairenn be brought within the royal ramparts of Tara. The king seated her beside him, saying, "From this day onward, you are a slave no longer but the Queen of Tara and the queen of my heart. For your son has taught me to honor what I have been ashamed to acknowledge and shown me the courage that belongs to a king."

He ordered that Mongfind be taken from Tara before her threats and demands could poison his ear once more and enslave him to do her will.

So as the poet had predicted, as the smith had judged and as the Goddess of the Land had proclaimed, Niall became King of Tara after his father's death, to be loved and honored by all who knew him.

LULLABY OF THE TRAVELING FAIRIES

One night in the glen, in the glen of Ball'comish,
The blackbird will come to build her own nest.
Sleep sound, dear child, the fairies will come to us,
Hush now, my baby, the bird I will call.

One night in Glen Rushen, up high in the mountains,
The falcon will come to build her own nest.
Sleep sound, dear child, the fairies will come to us,
Hush now, my baby, the bird I will call.

One night on the rocks of the high Spanish Headland,
The seagull will come to build her own nest.
Sleep sound, dear child, the fairies will come to us
Hush now, my baby, the bird I will call.

They'll come to Gordon, but there so conveniently
There will the little wren build her own nest.
Sleep sound, dear child, don't you fear those Fair Folk,
Hush now, my baby, the bird I will call.

Traditional Manx, translated by Caitlin Matthews. This is the song that mothers sing on the Isle of Man to help their children go to sleep.

THE MYSTERIOUS CLAW

WELSH

O nce upon a time in South Wales, so long ago that I cannot say when, young Pwyll was made Lord of Dyfed. On that very day, Pwyll decided to climb to the top of a nearby hill.

"What is the name of this place?" he asked Pendaran, one of his councillors.

"My lord, this is the Hill of Arberth. It is said that if a man of royal blood sits upon this hill, one of two things will happen. Either he will receive blows or he will see a great wonder."

Being among his friends and followers, Pwyll did not think it would be likely that he would receive blows from anyone there, so he said cheerfully, "I would be very glad to see a wonder." And he began to climb, accompanied by a handful of his men.

As he sat upon the summit of the hill, he looked down to the road below and saw a beautiful woman dressed entirely in gold, riding slowly upon a pale horse.

At the sight of her, he asked, "Does anyone know who she is?" His men

shook their heads, so he sent one of them to stop her and ask. By the time the man had reached the road, the woman had long gone past. However quickly the man followed her, he could not catch up, though it seemed that she was still riding slowly. Clearly the man would not be able to catch up with her on foot, so Pwyll sent another man after her upon horseback. But still the lady could not be overtaken.

The next day, Pwyll arranged for the fastest horse in the kingdom to be saddled and went and waited upon the hill. Again, the horsewoman came by and Pwyll's man rode swiftly after her, but however hard he rode, she kept ahead of him, still seeming to be riding slowly.

"There is clearly some meaning to this mystery," said Pwyll, feeling both excited and disturbed at the same time. Though he laughed and sang with his followers that night, he was also thinking. He was considering how he might find out who the lady was.

The next day he had his own horse saddled, and went to sit on the hill. When the lady once more came riding by, he spurred his horse to catch up with her. Pwyll was puzzled, for however hard he rode, she still remained the same distance ahead of him. When his poor horse could travel no farther, Pwyll called out, "Lady, in the name of the one whom you love the best, stop for me!"

The lady stopped her horse, turned and looked at him, with raised eyebrows. She turned her face so that he might see her. "You might have spared your

horse by asking me earlier!" she said.

Pwyll blushed for shame, but the lady was so beautiful that he took courage and asked her, "Where have you come from? And where are you going?"

"I am about my own business," she said mysteriously. "But I am glad to see you."

"Why have you come here?" he asked her, for he hoped that she had come because he had been sitting on the summit of the hill.

She smiled. "I have come to see you," she said. "My name is Rhiannon, daughter of Hefydd the Ancient, and I am being given in marriage to a man whom I hate. It is you I love, not him. What is your answer to that?"

Pwyll was delighted. "If I had all the women in the world to choose from, I would have chosen you first," he said. "When shall we be married?"

Rhiannon said, "Come to my father's court a year from tonight and we shall be wed."

Once they had parted, Pwyll could talk of nothing else but his betrothed. After a long year had passed, Pwyll and his men rode to the court of Hefydd the Ancient to claim Rhiannon. A great feast was prepared and everyone had begun to eat when a young nobleman entered the hall and greeted Pwyll.

"Lord," he said, bowing, "I have come to make a request."

Pwyll was feeling so happy that he said, "Whatever lies in my power shall be yours!"

Sitting beside him, Rhiannon hissed urgently, "Of all things, why did you say that?"

The nobleman smiled crookedly at her, saying, "Lady, he has promised before all these witnesses."

Then Pwyll knew he had made a dreadful mistake. Doubtfully he asked, "What do you want?"

"I want Rhiannon as my wife and I want the feast that you are enjoying," said the nobleman.

Pwyll was struck dumb with shock. Rhiannon whispered to him, "Say no more, for goodness sake! This is Gwawl, son of Clud, the man I was to have married!"

"What can we do?" wailed Pwyll.

"Listen to me," she said. "You must do as you promised, but there is a way through this, if you will do as I say."

Pwyll nodded miserably and listened to her plan.

"I am waiting, Pwyll," said Gwawl, impatiently tapping his foot.

Pwyll responded, "You shall have as much of your request as I can grant."

Rhiannon said to Gwawl, "This feast was prepared by myself and given to Pwyll's men, so it is not his to give. As for myself, you shall claim me in a year's time."

And Pwyll and Rhiannon parted for the second time.

A year passed, and Pwyll prepared to enact Rhiannon's plan. On the appointed day, he set out in disguise to the court of Hefydd the Ancient, where he saw his beautiful Rhiannon sitting next to the hated Gwawl.

Pwyll was unrecognizable as the Lord of Dyfed, for he and his men were dressed as beggars. Boldly he strode up to the high table and announced, "Lord, I have a request!"

Gwawl looked down at the filthy stranger, "Because it is my wedding day I will grant whatever request is reasonable."

Pwyll produced a leather bag. "Lord, I am hungry. I ask only that my bag be filled with food."

Gwawl granted this with a wave of his hand and the servants began to pile food into the bag. But however much food they put into it, the bag never seemed to be full. Now, this was no ordinary bag but belonged to Rhiannon, and she had given it to Pwyll for this purpose.

"Friend, it seems that your bag is hungrier than yourself!" cried Gwawl. "Will it never be full?"

"Lord, it is true that my bag will only be satisfied if the richest nobleman here stands upon the food in the bag and says "Enough has been put inside."

Rhiannon leaned over to Gwawl and said, "My lord, since you will soon have my dowry, no man at this feast is richer or more noble than yourself."

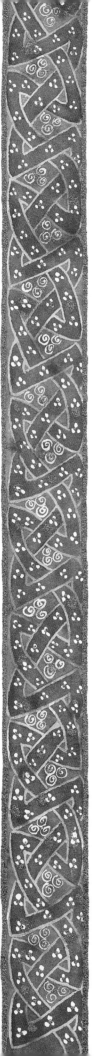

Gwawl rose proudly and stood upon the food in the bag with as much dignity as he could. But as soon as he did so, Pwyll quickly drew the sides of the bag up and tied them tightly together over Gwawl's head and blew his horn. In rushed his men with clubs in their hands.

"What's this in the bag, Lord Pwyll?" they asked.

"Just a wild beast," said Pwyll. And the men began to strike the bag with their clubs until Gwawl cried out for them to stop.

Hefydd the Ancient exclaimed, "This is no way to treat a nobleman!"

"Indeed, no!" said Pwyll. "What shall we do now?" he asked Rhiannon, whose idea this had been.

"Make Gwawl promise that he will give gifts to all the bards and any beggars at this feast, and that he will make no legal claims against you or seek any further revenge upon us."

In front of witnesses, Gwawl quickly promised all that they asked, and hobbled away much bruised. Then the feast began all over again and Rhiannon was finally married to Pwyll, and there was great rejoicing.

Pwyll brought Rhiannon to his house at Arberth where they lived peacefully for three years until the people of Dyfed began to complain that the Lady of Dyfed had given Pwyll no children. He should choose another wife, they said, and send Rhiannon away. Pwyll asked them to be patient, and a year later, on May Eve, Rhiannon gave birth to a fine little boy. That night, the women who looked after the mother and baby fell asleep. When they awoke before dawn, the baby was missing.

"Pwyll will blame us for this and burn us to death!" they wailed.

One of them had a dreadful idea to cover up the fact that they had carelessly fallen asleep. "Let's kill one of the deerhound's puppies and make it look as if Rhiannon has killed her own child!"

A little later that morning, they rushed into the hall screaming and crying that Rhiannon had killed the baby. Everyone crowded into the chamber where Rhiannon lay asleep, only to find a terrible sight. Blood and bones were strewn about the bed and the floor, and Rhiannon's face and hands were covered with blood. Amid the grief and confusion, Rhiannon awoke.

However many times they accused her of murder, Rhiannon could only deny the charge. She begged the lying women to tell the truth, promising that she would protect them, but they were frightened at what might happen and so they stuck to their lies.

Pwyll was heartbroken. He knew that his wife could not have done this terrible thing, but the people and his councillor were convinced of her guilt. He told them that he would not have her killed, since she had borne him a son, but that some other punishment must be devised. The judges conferred and then decided what should happen to her

They said that her punishment was that for the next seven years she must stand by the mounting block at the front gate of the court. There she must stop anyone who came in and tell them the shameful story of what she had done, and then she must offer to carry all guests into the hall on her own back.

And so Pwyll and Rhiannon were parted for a third time, for he was no longer permitted to treat her as his wife, nor to talk to her directly. He grieved as Rhiannon stood out in the yard in all weathers, greeting guests with the story of her baby's murder and offering to act as a mount to anyone who chose.

Very few people would actually consent to ride upon her back, but occasionally some unkind and curious guest would enjoy treating the wife of Lord Pwyll as if she was a horse. In this way nearly five years went by.

Now, far away in woodland Gwent, there lived a good man called Teyrnon. He had a very strange and mysterious problem. He owned a fine mare that would give birth to a foal every May Eve. But, every year, while he watched and waited for its birth, Teyrnon would fall asleep. When he awoke, the foal would have disappeared.

That very year, Teyrnon decided that this had gone on long enough and, armed with a covered lantern and his sharp sword, he sat up in the stables to see what would happen. The mare foaled that May Eve, and Teyrnon was uncovering the lantern to admire the fine little colt when he heard a sound that made him tremble, and through the window, he saw a mysterious claw come in and seize the foal. Teyrnon raised his sword and hacked off the end of the arm holding the foal. There was a terrible scream and he ran outside to make sure that the owner of the monstrous claw was dead. But there was nothing outside. When he re-entered the stables to check that the foal and its mother were all right, he found a sturdy baby wrapped in fine clothes.

He went and told his wife what had happened, showing her the baby. Neither of them could understand what had occured, but it was clear that the baby was from a noble family. Teyrnon's wife had no child of her own and she begged her husband to keep the boy. They called him Gwri Golden Hair and raised him as their own. By the age of one, he could walk. By the age of two, he looked as if he was six years old. By the age of four, he could look after horses and ride them well. The foal that had been nearly snatched by the mysterious claw also grew and in time became his own horse.

Now, news of Rhiannon's punishment had spread all over Wales but Teyrnon had not realized its significance until someone said how much Gwri resembled the Lord of Dyfed. At once Teyrnon knew how wrong it was for him to keep Pwyll's child and how much suffering Rhiannon had undergone.

He and Gwri set out the next day to Dyfed. When they came to the gate, there was Rhiannon sitting by the mounting-block.

She stopped them, saying, "Good guests, go no farther until you hear the story of how I killed my own son with my own hands. My punishment is to carry you both into the hall on my back," and she bent down to the ground.

With tears in his eyes, Teyrnon refused and raised her up, saying, "Lady, come with us, for I have a tale to tell." And together they went into the hall to meet Pwyll and his council, and Teyrnon told them about the mare and the foal and the mysterious claw, and how Teyrnon had raised the boy, who they called Gwri.

Teyrnon bowed to Rhiannon, saying, "When I heard of your sorrow, I could not keep him any longer. Lady, surely this is the boy who you are supposed to have murdered? Is there anyone here who will deny it?"

The council muttered together, "This must be Pwyll's son!"

Rhiannon breathed a great sigh of relief. "At last my trouble is over!"

Pendaran, the councillor, said, "Lady, you have named your son well! Let him be called Pryderi, son of Pwyll."

Now "pryder" is Welsh for "trouble," and Rhiannon was unhappy at giving her son such an unfortunate name. "Surely, the name that he has now suits him better?"

But Pwyll said, speaking to Rhiannon for the first time in many years, "My love, it is only right that the boy should be given the name that his mother gave him when she knew he was safe and well."

And so Gwri was called Pryderi for the rest of his life. Teyrnon was richly rewarded, and the women who told the lies were severely punished.

As for Rhiannon and Pwyll, they were never parted again. But if you want to know more about the mysterious claw, then that is another story . . .

Healing Charm

Bride went out
In the morning early,
With a pair of horses:
One broke his leg,
With much ado,
That was apart.
She put bone to bone,
She put flesh to flesh,
She put sinew to sinew,
She put vein to vein.
As she healed that,
May I heal this!

*Scottish. If you've ever sprained or twisted or broken one
of your limbs, you'll know how painful it can be.
When the injury is tied up, here are some words to bring
swift healing.*

Notes On The Stories

The names in these stories are in Welsh, Breton or Gaelic (for the Irish and Scottish ones). These everyday languages are still spoken today and taught in schools, but they have their own rules of pronunciation, which I have given below.

The Lady From The Lake – Welsh

The Physicians of Myddfai were a real family, whose descendants are still living today. The healing ways that the Lady gave to Rhiwallon can be found in *The Herbal Remedies of the Physicians of the Myddfai*, edited by Dr. Derek Bryce, (Llanerch Enterprise, 1987). Some of these folk remedies we would still endorse, such as boiling parsley seed for the relief of gas, but applying hare's blood to the face to remove freckles is not to be recommended! However, the book does give good advice to healers of all ages, for it says that a healer should always be "kind, gentle, mild, meek, intelligent, wise and gentlemanly in act and deed, in word and conduct, being careful not to shame those whom he has to examine." The remedy that Rhiwallon gives to his father in the story is from this book. This story was first collected by Sir John Rhys in the nineteenth century from people living around Llandovery in central Wales, but this is my own version.

Llanddeusant – Hlan'THY'sant
Llyn y Fan Fach – Hlin uh van vach
Myddfai – MUTH'vie
Rhiwallon – Hree'WAHL-on
Rhys – Hrees

The Black Bull Of Norroway – Scottish

This traditional lowland story has always been one of my favorites. The heroine's patience and determination to find and rescue her beloved is rewarded in the end, but only after long trials. When we love someone, we will do everything in our power to support him or her, but sometimes it's hard to know how best to act. The title of the story reminds us that many of the people who settled in Scotland came from Scandinavia, but the content of the story is typical of Scottish folktales. Anyone from Scandinavia was referred to throughout the Gaelic-speaking world as a "Lochlander" – someone from beyond the seas.

The Boy Who Didn't Know – Breton

This tale explores the theme of the knowledge that is already inside us – not the recognized, academic kind, but the instinctive knowledge that we call "mother wit," which accompanies every animal, including human beings, though we seldom use it as much as we should. N'oun Doaré may not have known much, but he knew instinctively that the rusty sword and the old mare were meant for him. This story was collected by Luzel from Brittany in the mid nineteenth century.

N'oun Doaré – Noon DWAR'ay

The Cailleach Of The Snows – Scottish

The Gaelic word "cailleach" means "old woman" or "grandmother." Throughout the British Isles, lore and legends about the Cailleach are widespread, with every one of them agreeing that she is the longest-lived being in the whole land. The fact that she herds reindeer suggests that stories about her go back as far as the Ice Age, when there were indeed reindeer in Scotland. Bride is also an ancient goddess whose character has been associated with the fifth-century St. Brigid of Kildare, who, according to legend, traveled widely throughout the British Isles. These two great goddesses are brought together in this story because they are associated with the winter and spring months, and many of the stories about them are concerned with the softening of winter's rigor and the coming of spring. This story is one of my own devising, drawing widely upon the folklore of both goddesses who have fascinated me since I was young.

Cailleach – KAL'yach

The Slave Woman's Son – Irish

Niall Noígiallach, or Niall of the Nine Hostages, was an historical Irish king who died about 405 C.E. His heirs did indeed become kings after him. This is one of the many stories about the Celtic Goddess of Sovereignty, who calls herself "Flaitheas" or "Lordship." She is a personification of the land itself who appears throughout Irish legend from this early story right through the "aisling" or vision poems of the eighteenth-century Munster poets, when the traditional Gaelic-speaking poets of south-west Ireland envisaged her as a beautiful woman in need of a hero to champion Ireland to liberate her from the many wrongs that arose from British colonization. We perhaps know her best in the modern era through the depiction of Ireland as Cathleen ni Houlihan by the great poet and playwright, W. B. Yeats. The story of Niall of the Nine Hostages, King of Tara, is taken from *Echtra mac n-Echach Muigmedóin*, the full text of which can be found in *The Encyclopedia of Celtic Myth and Legend* by John and Caitlín Matthews, (Rider 2003).

Cairenn – KAR'en
Eochaid – YO'hee
Mongfind – MO'vin
Niall – NEYE'al
Sithchenn – SHEE'han

The Mysterious Claw – Welsh

For the Celtic peoples, the horse was one of their most important animals, not merely for mobility and warfare, but because it was sacred to the Goddess of Sovereignty (see the last story). Aspects of this long veneration survive to today, for, although we have long forgotten the reason, we never speak of a "white" horse, but rather of a "gray," out of ancient respect, nor does anyone in Britain eat horseflesh without the greatest repugnance. Rhiannon is a Welsh representative of the pan-European Celtic Horse Goddess, Epona. In this story she is a woman whose real nature is revealed when she is made to carry in guests upon her back, like a horse. There is an implicit joke in the Welsh meanings of Pwyll and Pryderi's names, which may be lost on the English reader: respectively they can mean "Mind" and "Anxiety." This story is called Pwyll, Prince of Dyfed, and is part of a longer sequence of stories from the *Mabinogion* (a collection of medieval Welsh stories). It concludes in the story of Manawyddan, son of Llyr, in which Rhiannon and Pryderi have further hair-raising adventures. The identity of the possessor of the mysterious claw is never established, but we may recall that the family of Gwawl, unlike Gwawl himself, never swore to the promises that Rhiannon made! For more background on the stories of the Mabinogion, see my book *Mabon and the Guardians of Celtic Britain* (Inner Traditions, 2002).

Arberth – AR-bearth
Dyfed – DUV'ed
Gwawl ap Clud – Gwowl ap klid
Gwri – GOO'ree
Hefydd – HEV'ith
Pendaran – Pen-DAR-an
Pryderi – Prud-ER'ee
Pwyll – POO'ihl
Rhiannon – Hree-ANN'on
Teyrnon – TIRE'non

Barefoot Books
Celebrating Art and Story

At Barefoot Books, we celebrate art and story that opens
the hearts and minds of children from all walks of life, inspiring
them to read deeper, search further, and explore their own creative gifts.
Taking our inspiration from many different cultures, we focus on themes that
encourage independence of spirit, enthusiasm for learning, and sharing of
the world's diversity. Interactive, playful and beautiful, our products
combine the best of the present with the best of the past to
educate our children as the caretakers of tomorrow.

Live Barefoot!
Join us at www.barefootbooks.com

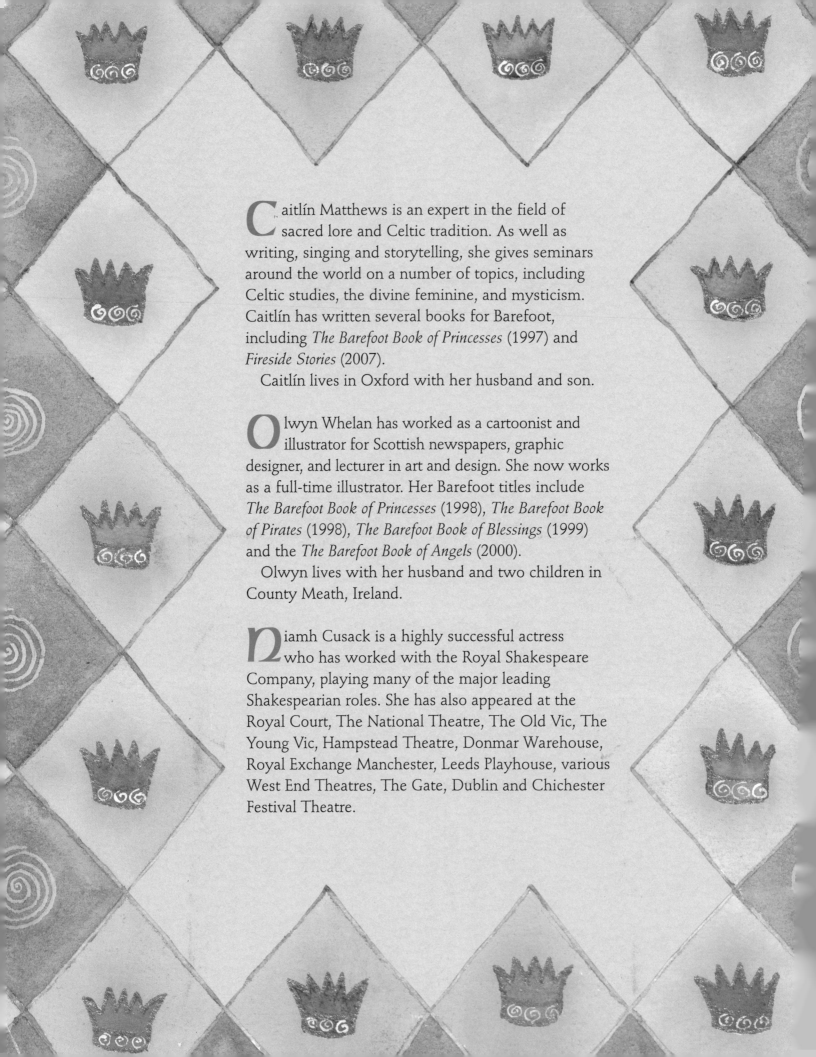

Caitlín Matthews is an expert in the field of sacred lore and Celtic tradition. As well as writing, singing and storytelling, she gives seminars around the world on a number of topics, including Celtic studies, the divine feminine, and mysticism. Caitlín has written several books for Barefoot, including *The Barefoot Book of Princesses* (1997) and *Fireside Stories* (2007).

Caitlín lives in Oxford with her husband and son.

Olwyn Whelan has worked as a cartoonist and illustrator for Scottish newspapers, graphic designer, and lecturer in art and design. She now works as a full-time illustrator. Her Barefoot titles include *The Barefoot Book of Princesses* (1998), *The Barefoot Book of Pirates* (1998), *The Barefoot Book of Blessings* (1999) and the *The Barefoot Book of Angels* (2000).

Olwyn lives with her husband and two children in County Meath, Ireland.

Niamh Cusack is a highly successful actress who has worked with the Royal Shakespeare Company, playing many of the major leading Shakespearian roles. She has also appeared at the Royal Court, The National Theatre, The Old Vic, The Young Vic, Hampstead Theatre, Donmar Warehouse, Royal Exchange Manchester, Leeds Playhouse, various West End Theatres, The Gate, Dublin and Chichester Festival Theatre.